Shrek the Third: The Movie Storybook
Copyright © 2007 by DreamWorks Animation L.L.C.
Printed in the United States of America.

Library of Congress catalog card number: 2007920946
ISBN-13: 978-0-06-122871-1 — ISBN-10: 0-06-122871-0

Typography by Rick Farley
❖
First Edition

DREAMWORKS®
SHReK THE THiRD™

The Movie Storybook

Adapted by Alice Cameron
Illustrated by Larry Navarro

HarperEntertainment
An Imprint of HarperCollins*Publishers*

"Prepare, foul beast, to enter into a world of pain!" Prince Charming threatened.

"*Grrrrr!*" went an actor in an ogre costume as he lurched onstage. The audience erupted into applause, as an annoyed Prince Charming struggled to concentrate.

The audience mocked him further, laughing and throwing fruit.

This wasn't how it was meant to be, Charming thought. He was supposed to have it all—the girl, the castle, the adoring subjects—and yet here he was, performing his tragic tale night after night at a third-rate dinner theater.

eanwhile, in the majestic castle of Far Far Away, Shrek and Fiona were filling in for Fiona's father, the ailing King Harold. Shrek was *not* happy about it. Wearing silly, frilly costumes, the pair prepared for a royal ball.

"I don't know how much longer I can keep this up, Fiona," Shrek complained.

Just then Shrek got an awful itch . . . on his behind! Scratching that itch had terrible consequences when his belt flew off, hitting Donkey.

Donkey fell into a lady who pushed him into a guard. The guard dropped an ax that knocked over a vase that spilled water on Fiona. Shrek then stumbled and sent a page flying. The party was ruined!

Soon after, Shrek and Fiona were summoned to King Harold's room.

"I'm dying," said the king.

But there was business to attend to first.

"This kingdom needs a new king. You and Fiona are next in line for the throne," he said.

What? King! Shrek didn't want to be king. He wanted to go home to his smelly swamp. There *had* to be someone else!

And there was . . . a cousin named Arthur. The king proclaimed this last bit of royal information, and then he croaked.

Despite the passing of Far Far Away's beloved king, things were normal at The Poison Apple Inn . . . until an unwelcome intruder arrived.

Prince Charming had come with one mission: to gather support from the fairy-tale villains. He knew they, too, had been wronged, and that the villains probably wanted more out of life. He had a plan to get them on his side.

"Someone decided *we* were the losers, but there are two sides to every story, and ours has not been told. So who wants to join me? Who wants their happily-ever-after?" Charming asked.

The villains cheered! Charming was right! They would help him take over Far Far Away.

Determined to avoid being king, Shrek, along with Donkey and Puss In Boots, prepared for his quest. The mission: to find and bring back the next heir to the throne!

At the docks Donkey kissed his wife, Dragon, and said good-bye to his baby Dronkeys. Fiona was there, too; and she had some news she *had* to tell Shrek. And so Fiona shouted across the water to his ship.

"Shrek, I'm pregnant. You're going to be a father!"

Shrek smiled back at Fiona. But he'd never been more scared in his life.

At long last the group reached their destination, a high school named Worcestershire Academy. Shrek, Donkey, and Puss marched through the campus and watched a tall, good-looking knight easily defeat a smaller, less impressive student on horseback.

"Strong, handsome, face of a leader. Doesn't that look like a king?" Shrek asked.

But Shrek was wrong. It turned out the winner of the joust was not Arthur at all. He was the scrawny kid who'd *lost* the match! Arthur hurried off, away from the big, green ogre and his sidekicks.

uss led them into a nearby gymnasium, where Worcestershire's new mascot was being announced.

"Come on out, Arthur, I know you're in here!" Shrek called.

"We need to be getting going. You're the new king of Far Far Away," he added.

"Artie a *king*?" one kid called. "More like the Mayor of Loserville!"

The crowd erupted in laughter. But Artie didn't care. He couldn't believe his luck! So long, high school, with its wedgies, jousting competitions, and cliques.

"Enjoy your stay here while I rule the free world," Arthur declared.

hile Shrek, Donkey, Puss, and Artie prepared to board their ship back to Far Far Away, the princesses and fairy-tale creatures threw Fiona a baby shower.

"It's present time!" Snow White sang.

"Ta-*dah*!" Pinocchio called out, spinning to reveal a baby carrier with a cozy, toasty Gingerbread Man placed inside.

"You know the baby's gonna love it, because I do!" Gingy said.

"Oh, you guys, that's so sweet! Thank you," Fiona replied.

But things *outside* the castle weren't all cake and cookies.

"Onward, my friends, to our happily-ever-afters!" Charming called.

The fairy-tale villains had formed an army intent on taking over Far Far Away. Down from the sky swooped Prince Charming, Cyclops, and the evil witches atop broomsticks. Evil trees dropped like bombs, parachuting to the ground.

After invading downtown Far Far Away, they headed for the castle, terrifying villagers all along the way.

reparing for the oncoming attack, the fairy-tale creatures barricaded the door with heavy furniture. The party was officially over!

As Gingy and the others stayed back, Fiona, the princesses, and the queen ran through a hidden passageway behind the fireplace. Just as the secret door slid back into place, Charming, flanked by Captain Hook and Cyclops, burst into the room.

"Where are Shrek and Fiona?" Charming yelled, pointing at Pinocchio's chest.

Just then a little pig squealed their whereabouts.

"He's bringing back the next heir?" repeated Charming.

"No!" lied Pinocchio, his nose growing and growing.

En route to the castle, Donkey and Puss told Artie all about being king.

"You'll be living in the lap of luxury. They've got the finest chefs ready to take your order and royal taste testers so you don't get poisoned," Donkey explained.

"And bodyguards willing to lay down their lives in devotion to you," Puss added.

Poison? Bodyguards? Artie had heard enough. Maybe high school wasn't *all* that bad after all. So he tried to turn the boat around, but Shrek wouldn't let him. The two wrestled for the ship's wheel until the boat lost control and crashed into land.

The group staggered onshore, and Artie took off into the wood. He came upon a cottage and pounded on the door.

"Help, help, HELP!" he yelled, as an old man answered. "Mr. Merlin?"

It was Worcestershire's former magic teacher.

The shipwrecked group bickered till Merlin cut them off.

Insisting that they work out their differences, Merlin built a roaring fire. Artie looked and saw himself as king of a castle that had teeth and wanted to eat him! Shrek saw it as an opportunity to have a quality ogre-to-new-king chat.

"I know it's hard to believe with my charm and good looks, but people used
to think of me as a villain," Shrek said. "But just because people call you a terrible
monster doesn't mean that you are one."

Artie understood what Shrek meant. Sure, the kids at school called Artie names,
but it didn't mean he *was* those things.

eanwhile, Fiona, the queen, and the princesses wandered through the catacombs beneath the castle.

"This place is filthy," complained Cinderella.

"This isn't working for me," agreed Snow White. Finally, Fiona found a ladder that led into the castle courtyard.

Just then Rapunzel ran off in the direction of the castle.

"Come on, this way!" she called, skipping right into the arms of Charming.

"Say hello to the new queen of Far Far Away," Charming declared.

Rapunzel had led the ladies right into a trap!

"Shrek will be back soon, Charming, and you'll be sorry," Fiona promised.

Things weren't any better for Shrek and company. They woke up at Merlin's camp to find pirates and evil trees attacking them!

"*Ahhhhhh!*" screamed Donkey, summing up the situation.

The pirates charged, swinging in on tree branches as Captain Hook played his piano menacingly.

"King Charming has something special in mind for you, ogre," he warned.

Puss quickly drew his sword and fought back as Artie tripped a pirate with his foot. But soon Donkey, Puss, and Artie were surrounded. Shrek rushed to their rescue. He defeated the pirates and saved his friends.

hrek had to get back to Far Far Away. Now! Artie knew that Merlin could use magic to get them there, but first he had to convince him. So Artie tried the only trick he knew—he cried. The tears were fake, but Merlin didn't know that! He agreed to zap them back to Far Far Away.

As Shrek, Artie, Donkey, and Puss entered downtown, they saw its new name: GO GO AWAY. Graffiti was everywhere. Pinocchio was imprisoned as a coin-operated puppet.

This was the place Artie had heard so much about?

Pinocchio told Shrek that Charming had taken over Far Far Away and was planning something terrible for that night. And worst of all—Pinocchio reported that Fiona was imprisoned.

Shrek, Donkey, and Puss tricked their way into Charming's dressing room. Suddenly guards ran into the room. The good guys were outnumbered.

"This *boy* is the new king?" Charming asked incredulously, looking at Artie.

Shrek formed a quick plan that would hurt Artie's feelings, but wouldn't get Artie hurt for *real*.

"You aren't the real king. I am," Shrek told Artie. "I just needed some fool to replace me and you fit the bill. So just go!"

Artie was hurt. Artie was confused. But he knew when he wasn't wanted. The guards released him, and Artie walked away, his head hanging down.

Held inside a prison cell, the princesses whined and complained just as Donkey and Puss were thrown in with them.

"Charming's got Shrek, Princess. And he plans on killing him in front of the whole kingdom!" Donkey explained.

The group needed a way out, and fast. Before anyone knew what was happening, the queen took a deep breath and head-butted a huge hole in the wall.

"Well, you didn't think you got your fighting skills from your father, did you?" the queen said.

"Okay, girls, let's take our happily-ever-afters back," Fiona declared.

Donkey and Puss rescued Dragon and the Dronkeys. Then they saved the fairy-tale creatures. Next they saw Artie . . . but Artie was still angry about being lied to.

"You both knew what was happening the whole time!" he shouted.

Donkey and Puss explained that Shrek was only trying to protect him. Artie understood.

Meanwhile, the strongest guards were no match for the ladies. They knocked Charming's men out two at a time as they advanced to the theater, just in time for the royal showdown.

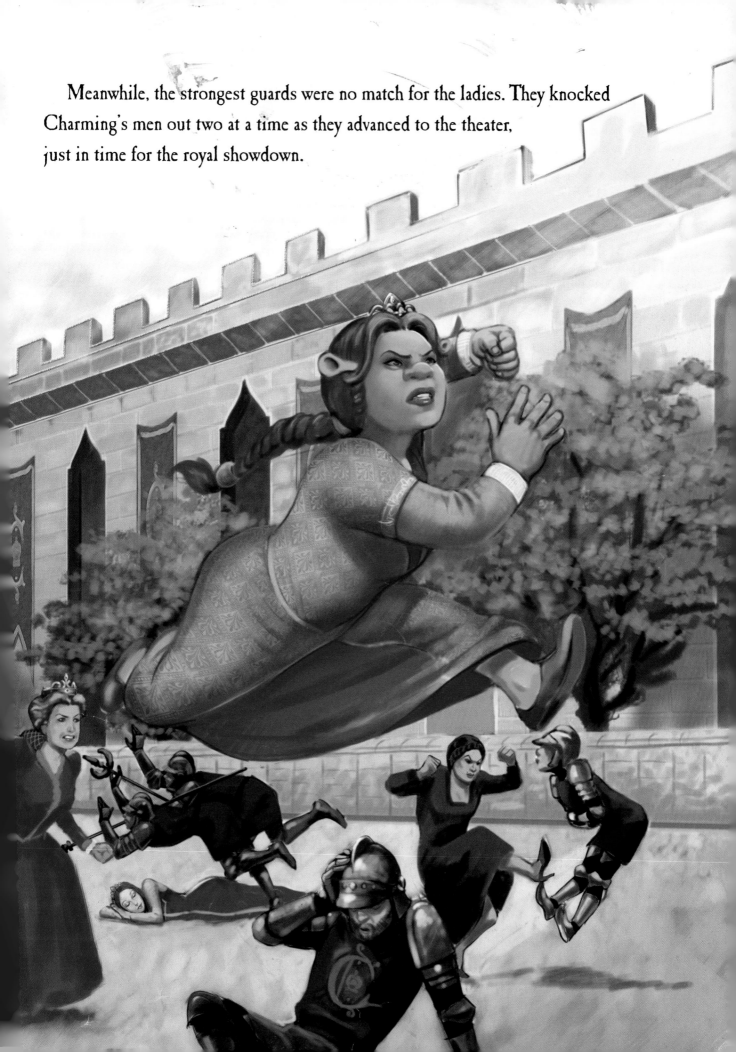

Charming's show, *It's a Happily-Ever-After, After All*, started as planned. The evil trees sang as the evil dwarves danced. Rapunzel stood high up in her tower while Charming sang about saving her from the awful ogre—Shrek.

A shackled Shrek rose up on the stage.

"You are about to enter a world of pain with which you are not familiAAAAAR," Charming sang with all his might.

"It can't be any more painful than your lousy performance," Shrek responded.

The audience laughed. But they weren't laughing with Charming, they were laughing *at* him.

egaining his composure, Charming continued with the show. *"Prepare, foul beast, your time is donnnnnne!"* he sang.

"Oh, not again. Have mercy. Kill me first," Shrek said mockingly.

Charming was angry now!

"Now you'll finally know what it's like to have everything that's precious to you taken away," Charming screamed and raised his sword, as the princesses and Fiona tore through the set decorations. The fairy-tale creatures jumped onstage, too, and prepared to do battle against the villains.

"Do you want to take these shackles off so we can settle this ogre-to-man?" Shrek asked.

Charming clapped his hands. The fairy-tale villains entered the stage and captured Fiona, the princesses, and their fairy-tale friends.

"You won't ruin things *this* time, ogre. This is *my* happily-ever-after!" Charming declared.

It wasn't looking good for Shrek. Suddenly a voice called from the rafters.

"Hold it!" Artie said, jumping down and landing awkwardly.

"Do you want to be villains your whole lives? Didn't you ever want to be anything else?" Artie asked.

The group listened. An evil tree grabbed Charming and held on tight.

One of the evil trees spoke first.

"It's hard to come by honest work when the whole world's against you," he said, summing it up for the entire group.

"A good friend of mine told me that just because people *treat you* like a villain doesn't mean you *are* a villain," Artie said.

One by one the villains threw down their weapons and confessed their hopes and dreams. The headless horseman wanted to learn the guitar. The evil queen wanted to open a spa. Captain Hook wanted to grow daffodils.

Shrek signaled to Dragon, and she used her mighty tail to knock Rapunzel's tower on top of Charming. He was defeated! And Artie was responsible! All of the fairy-tale creatures hoisted King Artie on their shoulders. *"Art-ie! Art-ie! Art-ie!"* they cheered.

Before long, the babies arrived. Yes, there were three little ogre babies. Shrek and Fiona's swamp home was crowded and full of excitement.

Donkey and Puss paid frequent visits, as did the queen. And before long the formerly royal couple got into the swing of things: feeding and burping with efficiency. It wasn't the life Shrek originally imagined for himself. It was much, much better.